D1193949

RHAMON

Rhamon

RHAMON

A Boy of Kashmir

By
HELUIZ WASHBURNE

Pictured by
ROGER DUVOISIN

JUNIOR PRESS BOOKS
ALBERT WHITMAN
& CO
CHICAGO
1939

Lithographed in the U.S.A.

CONTENTS

PAGE
Fishing 17
Cooking Supper 22
Making a Garden 27
A Trip to the City 33
Thieves 41
The *Monarch* 47
The Garden of Happiness 53
The Big River 62
Celebration for the Rajah 70
Wonderful News 79
A Mountain Storm 85
The Fire-Breathing Monster 91
Rhamon Delivers the Perfume Jar 95
An Exciting Day in the Bazaar 100
Snake Charmers 110
All Is Well for Rhamon 116
Going Home with the Road Gang 120

FULL PAGE ILLUSTRATIONS

PAGE

Rhamon .... *Frontispiece*

On the river were little houseboats 19

She put a pot of rice over the burning coals 23

Slowly the boat would move forward, pulling the garden behind 31

They passed boats of every description 35

Rhamon climbed after his father up some dark and narrow stairs 39

Rhamon realized that these men were thieves 43

They sent the boat through the water with long, swift strokes 51

"Who made these great gardens, my father?" 55

She slid her boat out into the lake again 59

The bridge of shops in Srinagar 62

He was working on a large tray 67

Strung high up was the word WELCOME 75

Subro was smoking his hubble-bubble pipe 83

ILLUSTRATIONS — (*Continued*)

Lightning ripped the sky apart 87

Crowds of people passed him coming and going 103

The trickster was making the flames shoot out from his lips 107

Subro picked Rhamon up in his arms 123

To

A courageous young boy
in the Vale of Kashmir

RHAMON

Chapter I

FISHING

RHAMON was fishing. Squatting carelessly on a narrow board that reached from the window of the houseboat to the river bank, he dropped his line into the clear water beneath. In the dark shadows of the overhanging bushes he could see the flash of a silvery fish as it glided past.

Rhamon was a small brown-skinned Indian boy. He had a little twisted foot, so he limped when he walked. But no one noticed his limp because Rhamon was always smiling. And when he smiled his big, brown eyes danced and his white teeth sparkled. His clothes were not very fine, but he wore a splendid turban, made of many yards of white cotton cloth, wound around and around his head.

Rhamon had spent all his life in the beautiful Valley of Kashmir, high up in the Himalaya Mountains. Happy Valley it was called, for here was a clear lake with many fish. Bright-colored birds flitted through the trees, fruits of all kinds grew on the grassy slopes, sweet-smelling flowers dotted the fields. And piled up on all sides were the mighty mountains.

A great old river wound its way through the narrow valley. Where the ground was low the river flooded over it and ran along in little winding canals. Small trees grew on the marshy banks and made feathery lace-like patterns

On the river were little houseboats

against the blue sky. On the lake, the river, and the canals were little houseboats where people lived. Rhamon's home was one of these houseboats on the water. It was not a large houseboat, and the roof was only a thick layer of woven reeds. Inside, it was barely high enough for his father to stand up straight without bumping his head. Ever since he could remember, Rhamon had been able to run along the narrow boards that stretched the length of the boat just outside the windows, and he had never fallen into the water.

Rhamon's father, Subro, was squatting on the deck of the houseboat, enjoying the sunshine and smoking his big water pipe that stood on the floor before him. As he puffed, the water in the glass jar bubbled and gurgled. And the blue smoke curled and twisted in the lazy breeze. Subro was a tall dark man with a black curly beard. He wore long white clothes that rustled as he walked. When he was angry his brown eyes were dark and fiery, but now as he smiled at Rhamon they twinkled and were full of fun.

Fishing was good today. Rhamon gave his pole a jerk, and up came a little silvery fish, twisting and wiggling and glittering in the sunlight. In went the hook again and up came another fish. And then another! Rhamon grew excited, for he had never known the fish to bite so fast. It wouldn't be long, he thought, before he had a good pailful all ready for supper.

He threw in his line again and waited. Soon he felt a fish take hold. He would land this fellow in a hurry. He gave a big jerk, and—splash! over he went backwards, line, fish and all! Subro jumped to his feet and ran to the rescue. When Rhamon was dragged to the deck, his turban was over one ear, and his clothes were wet and soggy. But his eyes were twinkling and his white teeth showed in a merry grin.

Chapter II

COOKING SUPPER

Rhamon's mother quickly stripped off his wet clothes and wrapped him in a warm blanket. Then he made himself comfortable in a corner of the houseboat and watched her cook the evening meal over a little charcoal fire.

First she lit one or two small pieces of charcoal and blew on them until they were glowing

She put a pot of rice over the burning coals

red. Then she placed other pieces on top and kept on blowing. Soon the fire was going and she put a pot of rice over the burning coals.

Rhamon's mother was little and very pretty. Her large dark eyes were half shaded by long, black lashes. Big silver rings were fastened through her ears, and from these hung many silver bangles that touched her shoulders. She wore heavy silver bracelets around her slender wrists.

Below her baggy white trousers silver anklets clinked when she walked. She even wore rings on her toes, for she always went barefoot. While she worked she sang, and Rhamon loved to listen. Her voice made music like the soft lapping of the water and the throbbing song of the bulbul bird.

While the rice was boiling, Rhamon's mother made the *chupatties* for supper. She pulled off a little wad of the dough she had mixed, and spread it out into a thin round cake. Then she rolled it up, twisted the roll around and patted it out flat once more. It was ready to be cooked then, so she dropped it on a dry hot griddle and set it over the fire. When the fire grew low she added more charcoal and blew on it to keep it hot. While the first *chupatti* was cooking she rolled out the next one. But always she watched the one on the fire. When it began to curl around the edge and turn brown, she quickly flopped it over to cook on the other side.

Rhamon liked these hot *cnupatties*, and it made him hungry to smell them cooking. When supper was ready his mother set a tray before him on the floor. On it were a bowl of rice, a plate of the fish Rhamon had caught, and a second bowl filled with curded milk. Using his fingers and bits of *chupatti* to scoop up his food, he soon had finished it all. Subro, squatting beside him on the floor, had another tray. And while they ate, Rhamon's mother cooked more *chupatties.*

That night when the sun went down, Rhamon watched the mountains change from gold to deep rose, then purple. And finally as night crept over the valley, they seemed to be draped in velvety blackness. Then he watched the stars come out one by one in the dark sky. Rhamon never felt alone when the stars were shining. The big moon slid up from behind the mountains and made a yellow path across the water to his very window.

Lying in his narrow bed, Rhamon listened to the night sounds—the evening call of the bulbul, the splash of the water against the boat, and the cry of the heron from the reed beds in the river. Before he went to sleep he watched for the one light that gleamed from a lonely temple on the top of a nearby hill.

Chapter III

MAKING A GARDEN

In the morning when Rhamon looked out of his window, he could see all around him the great peaks of the Himalaya Mountains. There were rows and rows of them, one beyond the other, till the last ones seemed like purple shadows in the distance.

In the winter they were snow-covered and

dazzling in the sunlight. In the early spring the lower slopes were brown, and long white fingers of snow reached down their rocky sides. Sometimes they were bathed in rain and their tops were lost in the billowy clouds. Now they had turned a soft green, and pink and white fruit trees blossomed at their feet.

Rhamon loved to watch the morning sunlight paint the snowcaps in magic colors and creep down the mountainsides to light the valley.

Looking deep into the water, Rhamon thought there must be two worlds—the right-side-up world where the mountains and trees stretched up into the sky, and the upside-down world which he glimpsed in the water, mountains and trees reaching downward.

Through the window Rhamon could see Subro working on the family patch of floating garden. Ever since Rhamon could remember, a garden had floated beside their houseboat, but he was very proud of this one because he had helped his father to make it.

First Subro had dragged the mud up from the bottom of the lake with long tongs. Then Rhamon had helped him mix the mud with twigs and shape it into big round clumps. They had let these dry in the sun. Later, when they had enough of them, they had bound the clumps together with long reeds to make a sort of raft. Now the garden was all finished, and ready to be planted.

So it would not drift away, Subro had stuck a great pole through it down into the muddy bottom of the lake. But if Subro grew tired of the river and the friendly little canals and wished to move his floating home to some more open spot, he could also move this floating garden. He would just take up the pole that held it fast and tie a rope around one end of the garden. The other end of the rope he would fasten to a ring in the deck of the houseboat.

Rhamon had often helped his father move their boat out into the lake. Standing at the front of the houseboat Subro would take a long pole and sink one end away down to the bottom of the river. Then, putting his shoulder against the pole, he would lean forward and shove and shove while walking along the boards toward the back end of the boat.

Slowly the boat would move forward, pulling the garden behind. Then he would take the pole out and go to the front, shove it in again and once more walk the length of the boat. Rhamon's pole was lighter than his father's, but he would follow along behind him, pushing with all his strength.

After a long time of poling like this the boat would be out in the big Dal Lake. Then Subro would always say, "Be careful, my son. The water here is very deep in places." And Rhamon would laugh. He would not fall in!

This morning Subro was planting cucumbers and melons in the garden. As soon as Rhamon had finished his breakfast, he ran out to help his father before the sun grew hot.

They worked until all the seeds were planted.

Slowly the boat would move forward, pulling the garden behind

Then Subro looked up and said, "This morning I am going to the city. Would you like to go with me, Rhamon?" A broad smile was Rhamon's only answer, as he dashed for the houseboat to get his sandals and rewind his turban.

Chapter IV

A TRIP TO THE CITY

Subro had a small, flat boat called a *shikara.* He kept it tied to his houseboat. It was long and narrow, pointed at the ends, and lay close to the water. Instead of oars, it had long-handled paddles with heart-shaped ends. Subro used it to visit his friends on other houseboats or to go to the city of Srinagar. Usually he paddled it himself, but when he was in a hurry he took his brothers Ibrahim and Ramzana to help him.

This morning he was taking his son. When Rhamon came out he jumped down into the back end of the *shikara* beside his father. Taking up their paddles they worked together with long quick strokes. Each stroke ended with a jerk that shot the boat forward through the water.

Rhamon made up his mind that when he was a man he would have his very own *shikara*—a splendid big one with fine carving, soft cushions inside and a place for six oarsmen.

On their way down the river they passed boats of every description. There were *shikaras* like their own, skimming swiftly over the water, merchant boats, dugouts loaded with vegetables, slow-gliding grain barges, and some being poled along by a man or woman who stood balancing far out on the tip.

Rhamon enjoyed these trips with his father to Srinagar. There was much to see and do there, and today he had a few *annas* to spend for sweets in the bazaars. Subro took his bubbling water pipe with him, for he was sure to meet

They passed boats of every description

his friends in the city. They would smoke and visit together before he returned.

Rhamon had his friends too. First he went to see Aziz, the old shoemaker, who had the little shop on the corner. Aziz made beautiful red leather slippers with curving pointed toes. Rhamon loved the nice leathery smell and the smooth feel of the big, colored skins that hung on the wall. He stayed a long time with the old man, listening to the stories he wove as he made wonderful patterns on a pair of shoes.

"These are for our great Rajah, the King," said Aziz, holding up the slippers and looking at them proudly. "He is coming here soon to his summer palace. There will be a great celebration in his honor. People will take him gifts of welcome. And these shall be my present. Allah be praised!"

The Rajah coming! The great King who lived in the beautiful palace! Rhamon stood silent. All his life he had heard of the Rajah. He wished he might see him—just once.

As Rhamon turned to limp from the shop, the old shoemaker smiled at him. "Some day," he said, "I shall make *you* a pair of slippers, and not even a king shall have a better pair!"

Before Subro returned to his home, he took Rhamon to the house of Subhanna, a rich merchant who lived down the river. The upper floors of Subhanna's big house hung out over the water and when Rhamon leaned from the high windows, he could see all that was happening on the water below.

Subhanna made beautiful articles out of silver. But he sold many other things besides the ones he made himself. There were shelves and shelves of bells, big elephant bells that made a deep "C-L-I-N-G, C-L-A-N-G" as the great beasts walked. There were pretty brass camel bells and even tiny tinkly ones for the goats that clambered on the mountainsides.

Rhamon saw an immense silver bowl standing on the table in one corner. Its handles were set with bits of gold and precious stones.

"This is a rare treasure," said Subhanna, touching it gently. "The Rajah is coming soon to his summer palace. There will be a great procession on the river, and hundreds of boats. People will bring him presents. And I shall take him this feasting bowl."

Rhamon sighed and turned to look at an old black gong that hung by the door. From a faraway temple it had come, where once it called the people to their prayers. Rhamon took up the padded stick and struck it. "Boo-o-o-o-o-o-o-o-o-o-o-o-m-m-m-m!" The great sound filled the room and seemed to echo from every wall. The frightened birds on the windowsill spread their wings and flew away to quieter places.

Rhamon climbed after his father up some dark and narrow stairs to still higher rooms. The steps were steep and made of rough stone and earth. On every floor were rooms and rooms filled with old and precious goods, but all of them were grey with dust. Subro wished to see one of the copper bowls.

Rhamon climbed after his father up some dark and narrow stairs

Subhanna clapped his hands to call a servant. Then the servant came with charcoal dust and water. Sitting on his heels on the floor he mixed these into a paste and spread it all over the bowl. Then he rubbed and rubbed with his hands until the copper sparkled and shone. Many bowls and vases the servant polished in this way for Subro. But before they left, Subro had finally bought a beautiful great perfume jar, made of copper worked with many colors.

"For whom do you buy that wondrous jar, my father?" asked Rhamon, as they paddled off in their *shikara.*

But Subro only smiled. Some day his son would know.

All the way home Rhamon was silent. He was looking ahead to the coming of the Rajah. If only he could think of some way by which he might see the great procession of boats on the river!

Chapter V

THIEVES

Late the next afternoon Rhamon was sitting on the narrow walk that ran around the outside of the houseboat. He was feeling happy, for his mother had just given him a freshly cooked *chupatti* wrapped about a bit of meat. As he munched it he dabbled his toes in the water and listened to the distant chiming of a temple bell. A mist hung over the river and the sun had almost set.

Suddenly he saw two men coming up the river, poling their boat very slowly and looking from side to side. Rhamon knew all the men of his own little village, but these were strangers. He wondered what they were doing, why they were going so slowly and looking around so carefully. He decided to watch them.

In a moment he saw them slide up beside a big piece of floating garden. Rhamon knew that it belonged to his neighbors who were away on a picnic across the lake. One of the men pulled out the long pole that held it in place. The other tied a big rope to one end of the garden. Suddenly Rhamon realized that these men were thieves from another village, come to carry away the garden.

Stuffing the last bit of *chupatti* into his mouth, Rhamon jumped quickly from his seat and slipped into the *shikara* that lay alongside the walk. In a moment he had untied the rope that held it to the houseboat. Soon he was shooting down the river toward the city of Srinagar.

Rhamon realized that these men were thieves

When he looked back he saw the men slowly poling their boat away. And the garden was going with them, back to their own village.

He paddled with all his strength. At the landing by the big bridge, Rhamon pulled the boat up on the shore. He must find his uncle, the Chief of Police. He hurried down one little street, turned a corner and ran up another. His foot was beginning to hurt, but he did not stop. When he finally reached the office he was almost out of breath. "Quick, Uncle, quick!" he panted. "Some men are stealing a garden!"

The big Chief of Police twirled his fierce black moustache, and rubbed his nose. Then he called loudly for two of his men. Rhamon shivered at the sound of his voice. It seemed to come rumbling up from the soles of his big red slippers. Settling his huge turban farther on his head, the Chief took Rhamon's hand and started off with long strides. Rhamon could hardly keep step with him, but he felt very proud. Was he not walking down the streets of the city with the Chief of Police? Everyone made way for them and salaamed, touching his hands to his forehead and bowing low.

"Jump into my boat," said his uncle. "We shall catch these thieves! My two men will follow in your *shikara*."

Away they sped, paddling swiftly past all the other boats. Suddenly Rhamon dropped his paddle and pointing up the river, cried, "There they are!" By now the thieves had seen the police also. Quickly they untied the garden they were towing behind them. In another minute they had disappeared into one of the many little canals.

"Now we have lost them!" exclaimed the Chief of Police, rubbing his big nose. "But by the grace of Allah, we shall catch them yet!"

"By the help of Allah perhaps, but by my help, too," thought Rhamon, for he was sure he would know those two men again if ever he saw them.

"And you can be glad you have saved the

man's garden, Rhamon," said his uncle, seeing the boy's disappointment. "You are clever. Some day you may be a policeman yourself."

"Yes," thought Rhamon. "Some day I shall be a Chief of Police, and have a big moustache like my uncle."

Chapter VI

THE MONARCH

Subro owned five or six of the finest houseboats on the river. In the summer he often rented them to people who came up into the mountains from the hot parts of India. The most beautiful one of all his houseboats was called the *Monarch*. Subro's own little houseboat was anchored not far from this one. So Rhamon saw everything that happened on board the *Monarch.* This summer an American man and his wife came to live on it. Rhamon called them the Sahib and Mem Sahib. When they arrived he heard his father say, "Sahib, the *Monarch* is a little floating palace. You shall live like a king on that boat."

And indeed Rhamon thought so too, for he had often been inside. He had felt the soft, thick carpets under his little bare feet. He loved the pretty colors of the embroideries that hung from the windows and covered the beds. And he liked to trace with his fingers the patterns of the wood carvings around the windows and doors.

Almost every day the river merchants poled their boats slowly up alongside the *Monarch* and looked in through the windows. Holding up some special treasure they would begin, "Mem Sahib will look? In all the world Mem Sahib will not find beads like these. Lady Sahib not buy, only look!" Their soft voices kept on and on until Mem Sahib looked.

Rhamon loved to talk with these merchants and see all the beautiful things they had brought to sell to the American Mem Sahib. There were soft shawls, gay wool embroideries, dainty bits of hand-worked silver, lovely boxes made of brass and crushed turquoise, beads and bracelets and fine wood carvings. Sometimes the merchants came up onto the tiny deck of the *Monarch.* Then Rhamon feasted his eyes on the piles of wonderful things that came tumbling out of their packs.

One day the American Sahib and his wife, the Mem Sahib, wished to cross the lake to a wonderful Persian garden that was known to everyone for its beauty. It was called Nishat Bagh, the Garden of Happiness. Subro had made everything ready for the trip. A beautiful big *shikara* floated beside the *Monarch.* It was long and slim and its carved prow rose gracefully out of the water. An awning was stretched over the middle part of the boat to keep off the hot sun. Hanging from this were little white side curtains, gay with bright red embroidery.

The Sahib and Mem Sahib stepped down inside and settled themselves on the big springy cushions. Bundles of lunch were stowed in the bottom of the boat. Subro's brothers, Ibrahim and Ramzana, and two other boatmen climbed into the back part. Rhamon was not going to be left behind, so he scrambled over the edge and took his place beside them. Picking up their paddles, they sent the boat through the water with long swift strokes.

Rhamon loved to help. Although his paddle was smaller than the men's, he could work as well as any of them. He never missed a stroke and his black eyes danced with delight.

Slender willow trees lined the banks of the tiny canals through which they wound their way. Ducks were paddling in the water. On the bank a wedding party was feasting and merry-making. Other boats glided quickly past them. In one a boy had a load of tree branches he had cut for the family fire. In another an old man

They sent the boat through the water with long, swift strokes

squatted out on the front tip, lazily smoking his hubble-bubble pipe. Sometimes the boats were poled by women dressed in ragged clothes, wearing many silver bracelets and heavy ear-rings.

When Rhamon rested from his paddling he liked to trail his hands in the cool water or pull up the pink and white water lilies that floated on the river. He could see their long stems through the clear water reaching down, down to the muddy bottom.

Chapter VII

THE GARDEN OF HAPPINESS

The boat came out of the river and crossed the big lake to the Garden of Happiness. Here it was made fast and everyone jumped out. Rhamon wanted to skip and dance, for he had never seen anything so lovely. Fruit trees were in bloom everywhere, standing white against the background of rough brown mountains; as if the snow from the highest peaks had blown down and settled on their branches, he thought.

Forgetting his lame foot, he ran limping along the great stretches of green grass, stopping to smell of the purple and yellow pansies that grew on the borders. He looked at his reflection in the pools of clear water, felt the spray of the sparkling fountains on his face, and laughed for joy.

Then he saw Subro coming up the path and asked him, "Who made these great gardens, my father?"

Subro answered, "Long ago, there was a noble Emperor named Jahanjir. He had a wife whom he loved with all his heart. To please her he made this beautiful garden. And here they often came to spend happy hours together. Players and singers filled the air with music. Dancing girls entertained them, slaves waited on them. And so it is called the Garden of Happiness."

A golden butterfly fluttered in the rainbow mist of the fountain and Rhamon started toward it.

"Who made these great gardens, my father?"

"Come now," called Subro, "and help unpack the lunch."

Rhamon ran back to the boat, and a big silver teapot was placed in his arms. He carried it up the path between the rows of giant Chenar trees, and stopped in the shade of one, bigger than all the others. Here spring beauties bloomed in the grass and made a pink and white carpet on which to set out the lunch.

"You were here when the Great Emperor came to this garden," thought Rhamon, looking up at the king of trees. "Your spreading branches kept him cool when the sun was hot, as they will keep us cool today. And if it rains, not a drop will fall between your thick leaves to wet us."

Ibrahim brought up a big cake and Ramzana came with bundles of sandwiches. The others brought more things, and soon the feast was ready.

There was good food for Rhamon to eat too, sweet cakes and a cup of warm tea. He took them back to the boat and sat there enjoying them. The cool breeze ruffled his hair and the warm sun beat on his back.

Soon another *shikara* slid slowly up beside him. It was poled by a little girl, and in the far front end sat her baby brother. Her dark hair was braided in with heavy black yarn to make it thicker, and hung far down her back in many pigtails. She wore large silver earrings and a tiny embroidered cap.

The little girl's big black eyes gazed longingly at the cake Rhamon was eating. She did not say a word, but Rhamon guessed what she wanted. He looked at his cake. It was not often he had a treat like this. And he had been eating it slowly to make it last. Then he looked into the little girl's dark eyes. Breaking his cake in half, he put a piece into her eager hand.

Then his heart was glad, for suddenly her face broke into a shy smile showing a row of white teeth. She stuffed the bit of cake into her mouth as if she were afraid Rhamon would ask to have it back. Then pushing the long pole deep into the water she slid her boat out into the lake again.

It was nearly dark when the party started home. Rhamon watched the sunset colors changing on the snowy mountains. As night came on he tried to count the stars reflected in the black water. The boat slid silently past the shadowy trees. Tiny lights appeared in the houseboats anchored by the shores. Sometimes the good smell of food cooking for the evening meal made Rhamon sniff and wrinkle up his little nose. He would like a big dish of spicy curry and some fluffy white rice.

How quiet everything was! Hardly a leaf stirred in the trees. There was no sound but the swi-i-i-*ish*! swi-i-*ish*! swi-i-i-*ish*! of the paddles and the drip of the water as it fell away from the blades.

Suddenly the stillness was broken by the rich voice of one of the boatmen. It was Ibrahim, singing an old Kashmir boat song. One by one

She slid her boat out into the lake again

the others joined him. Rhamon sang too, his voice rising clear and sweet above the men's deeper ones. Soon the night air was throbbing with the music. Then with his hands Subro began to beat the rhythm of the song on the side of the boat. Another boatman drummed on his paddle laid across his knees.

Sometimes their voices swelled to great shouts of joy. Then the boat sped swiftly through the water from the force of their strokes. But sometimes their song faded to a whisper of sadness and there were tears in their singing. Then the boat glided slowly through the darkness.

That evening the men gathered on Subro's little houseboat to sing together. They squatted on the floor in a circle and each held something to make music—a big red clay pot, a bell or a pair of homemade clappers. Ibrahim started a song. The others joined in, swaying from side to side. Then they began to ring the bells, clap the clappers, and beat on the pots.

Ramzana hit the open top of his pot with the

palm of one hand, and tapped the rounded side with the fingers of the other. It made a hollow drumming sound. Subro wore heavy silver rings on the ends of his fingers to make the sound sharper.

Rhamon was there too, of course, singing his heart out and shaking his head under his huge white turban. He loved this strange sweet music. He did not have an instrument to play, but he beat time on his father's knee with his hands and wrists. "Some day," he thought, "I shall be a man and then I shall play on one of the big red pots, and have silver rings on my fingers."

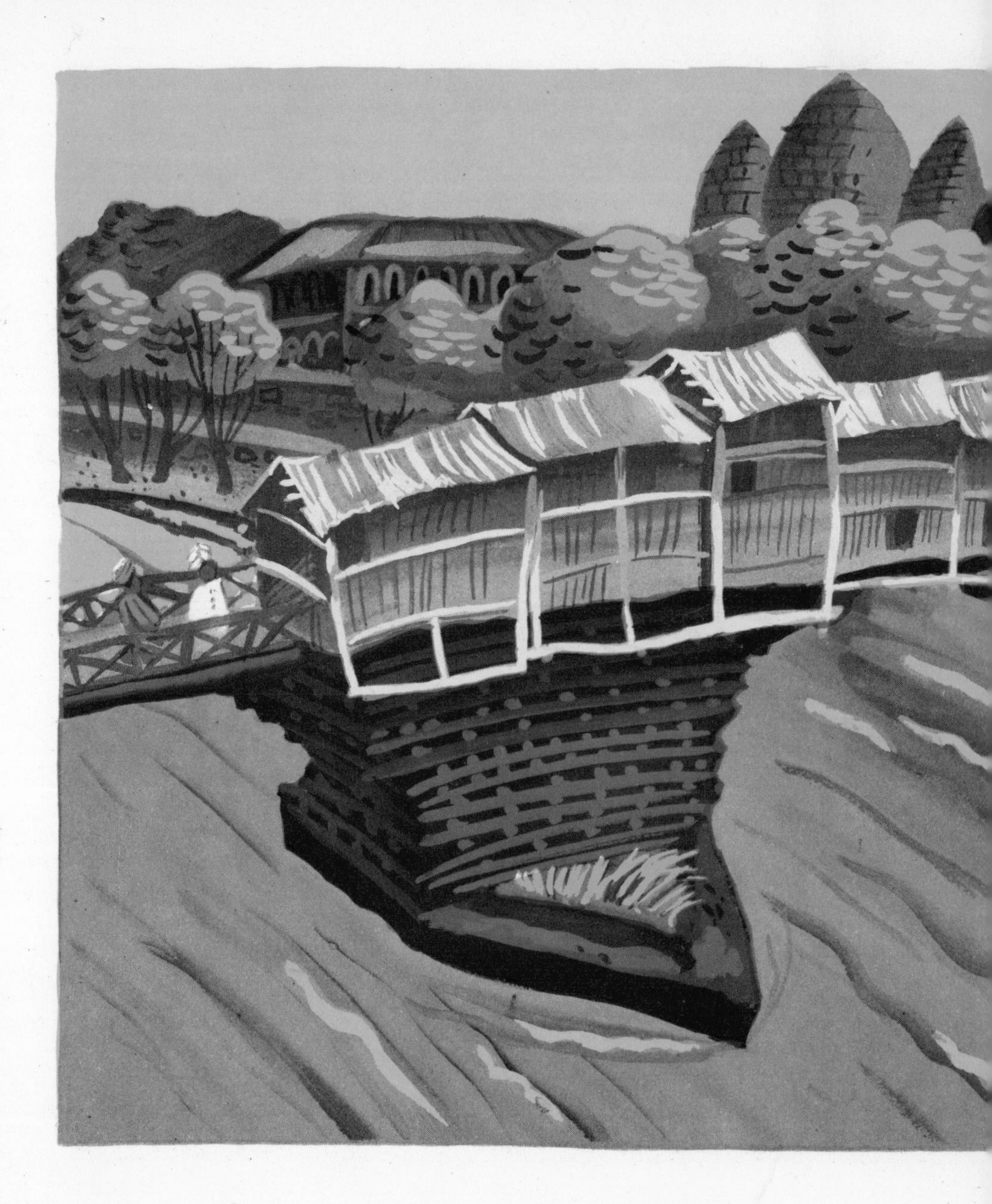

The bridge of shops in Srinagar

Chapter VIII

THE BIG RIVER

Seven great wooden bridges crossed the wide river that wound through the Valley. And the old, old city of Srinagar was spread along its banks. For hundreds of years people had walked across these bridges, or driven their wagons over them. For hundreds of years river boats of all sorts had been passing under them.

Rickety wooden houses clung to the river bank. The water lapped against their basements. Grass and red poppies grew out of their mouldy earth-covered roofs. Narrow little streets found their crooked way between the houses, down to the river's edge. Here they ended in crumbling wide stone steps.

Many of the streets in this old city were waterways, but the big river was the main street. Funny little shops faced the water front. Some of them had balconies where the merchants hung out their wares. Long strips of brightly dyed woolen cloth fluttered in the breeze. Silken carpets hung over the railings and glistened in the sunlight.

Here and there a temple or a royal palace rose above the tiny shops and dingy houses. Just beyond the third bridge and almost tumbling into the water stood an old wood-carving factory. Here Rhamon came the next morning with his father, who was to buy goods for the American Sahib.

There was great excitement all over the city of Srinagar this day. People were talking together everywhere—girls filling their water jars, men passing in boats on the river, women on the doorsteps. As Rhamon and his father paddled along they could hear what people said:

"Have you heard? Our King, the great Rajah, arrives tomorrow from his winter palace at Jammu. He comes up the river with a big procession of boats."

"Yes. My brother is his chief oarsman, and from him I have heard the Rajah has a new boat, larger and more beautiful than any before."

"For weeks I have seen men working in the gardens of the Summer Palace to make things ready for his coming."

"Tomorrow I shall go early and stand on the bridge, that I may see His Highness as the boats pass under. I shall be near enough to catch the sparkle of the big jewel on the front of his turban."

The *shikara* was made fast to the landing. Then

Rhamon and his father climbed up a steep flight of steps from the water and entered a dark and dingy building. It seemed hundreds of years old. An aged man led them between dusty piles of wonderful carved wood.

When Rhamon's eyes became used to the dim light, he saw half-naked men sitting cross-legged on the earth floor, busily carving. The boy stopped to watch one old man in the doorway. He was working on a large tray which he propped against the split log that served for a table. The pattern was so fine that he used a magnifying glass to see what he was doing.

"My child," he told Rhamon, "for many months have I worked on this tray. But now, praise Allah, it is about finished, and it shall be given to our King—the great Rajah—as a gift from one of his humble subjects."

"Everyone is making ready for the coming of the Rajah," thought Rhamon sadly, "everyone but me. And I shall not even see him."

Going home Rhamon helped his father pad-

He was working on a large tray

dle the boat. They passed back under the big bridges, one by one, gliding into the darkness and shooting out again into the golden sunlight. Rhamon watched the busy life on the shore and listened to the many sounds across the water.

He saw women coming down to the river's edge with great jars on their shoulders, and he heard them laughing and talking as they filled these jars with water.

"Slosh, slosh; whack, whack!" That was the laundryman washing his clothes in the river and beating them clean against the stone steps.

"Thud — thud — thud — thud!" That was a slow sound that Rhamon knew well, for he heard it every day. It came from a group of women on the shore who were pounding their rice. He watched them as they raised the heavy wooden poles and let them fall on the rice in the big stone bowls. It was hard and tiresome work. Often he wished he were big and strong enough to help his mother grind their daily rice.

The boat slid along and Rhamon did not

speak. "What troubles you, my son?" asked Subro, noticing his silence.

"Father, I should like to see the Rajah and take him a present," said Rhamon, with a great sigh.

"Allah is wise, and understanding. He is good to those who worship him faithfully," said Subro, smiling into his black beard.

Rhamon did not understand exactly what his father meant, but he was sure he had said all his prayers.

When they reached home, Rhamon was weary and his foot ached from climbing many stairs. So he sat down in his favorite corner to watch his mother cook the evening supper. As she rolled out the *chupatties* she sang, and Rhamon, listening, dropped off to sleep. He dreamed of the great Rajah with the blazing jewel on his turban. When his mother gently shook his shoulder to wake him for supper, he was happy, for in his dream the Rajah had smiled to him, to Rhamon, the little lame boy.

Chapter IX

CELEBRATION FOR THE RAJAH

On the great day of celebration there was no one in all the city so happy and so excited as Rhamon. Allah be praised, he was going to be one of the first people on the river to see the Maharajah when he arrived in his beautiful boat. He could not believe it was true. And all because he had told the police about the thieves.

His uncle was in charge of river traffic this day. As Chief of Police it was his duty to see that all the small boats kept to one side of the river, leaving the other clear for the great Rajah's procession. And Rhamon had been invited to ride with his uncle!

Not only that, but Rhamon was wearing his beautiful rose-colored suit with the gold embroidery on it, a splendid new turban, and best of all, a pair of fine red slippers with turned-up pointed toes—a gift from his friend Aziz, the shoemaker. He was fairly bursting with pride and happiness.

The river was alive with boats of every kind. Officers and other important people sat in fine *shikaras,* resting back on silken cushions. They were on their way to greet the Maharajah before he entered the city.

Rhamon sat proudly in the boat with his uncle. The Chief of Police looked bigger and more important than ever. His turban was larger, his uniform was finer and his moustache curled more fiercely. Was he not on the Rajah's business today?

The whole city was in holiday dress to pay honor to the Rajah. Bright shawls hung from the windows and fluttered in the breeze. Rhamon could read the words on the big banners stretched across the houses: "Welcome to the great Rajah. Long life to the King." Even the earth roofs of the houses were newly dressed, for many of them were covered with fresh grass, and the scarlet tulips growing there blazed in the sunlight. Flags and colored handkerchiefs were waving everywhere and the air was filled with cheering.

The Chief of Police was very busy giving orders and Rhamon was very busy watching what was happening all around him. Suddenly he saw a wonderful sight. Strung high up across the river was the word WELCOME in huge letters. But the letters seemed to be moving! Then as his boat came closer, Rhamon saw that they were made of real boys clinging to the long poles that formed the big letters.

"Look, Uncle!" he cried.

"Yes," replied the Chief of Police. "That is the way that their school gives a living welcome to the great Rajah."

"But if one of them lost his hold he would fall in the river!"

"Would you not gladly take that risk to honor your Rajah?" asked the Chief of Police.

Rhamon slowly nodded his head and they paddled on.

Looking down the glistening river Rhamon saw the first boats of the royal procession moving slowly forward. They were beautiful boats with painted sides, embroidered curtains and long lines of oarsmen in red uniforms.

Then Rhamon's eyes opened wide with wonder as he saw the great boat of the Rajah gliding toward him. It was longer than any boat he had ever seen. At the front and the back it rose out of the water like the spreading tail of a peacock. The central part was a tiny house with beautiful windows around the sides. Within sat the Rajah robed in wonderful colored silks and sparkling jewels.

Rhamon counted the oarsmen on the side of the boat nearest him. There were twenty-five of them! And he knew there were twenty-five on the other side, too. All were dressed in gorgeous scarlet uniforms. As they rowed, the oars on each side moved together like the wings of a great bird, now flashing in the sunlight, now dipping into the water.

"My!" thought Rhamon. "I would like to be one of those oarsmen. Someday I will be the head oarsman, like that one who is telling the others what to do. Then I shall take the great Rajah for a ride on the lake, for *I* will be the best oarsman in all of Kashmir."

Suddenly Rhamon noticed two men in a small *shikara* weaving their way among the closely packed boats on the river. He sat up with a start. Surely he remembered those faces. The two men who had stolen the garden! Tugging

Strung high up was the word W E L C O M E

at his uncle's sleeve, he cried, "The thieves! The thieves!"

"Where?" cried the Chief of Police, twirling his moustache furiously, and peering out over the crowd.

"There, just slipping under the bridge," said Rhamon excitedly.

"Ah," said his uncle, "they are on no good business here today. I will set my men to watch them." And he started paddling swiftly, giving orders as he passed.

Rhamon forgot about the thieves then, in watching the great procession which was coming closer and closer. Slowly the royal boats slid past the leaning houses, where faces peered from every window; past the steps on the water's edge, filled with people; and under the crowded bridge.

When the Palace was reached the Rajah's great boat stopped and all the other boats of his procession stopped, too. Hundreds of small boats circled and crowded around the Palace steps. Everyone was eager for a glimpse of the great Rajah. Then with one movement, the Rajah's fifty oarsmen stood their paddles up on end, making two rows of hearts down the length of the boat.

The Rajah was about to land. Now the people came bearing their gifts. With a beating heart Rhamon watched the beautiful things that were laid at his feet, a rug with colors that glowed like jewels, silken scarfs, soft rich wools, the beautiful tray made by the old wood carver, Subhanna's silver bowl with the gold and turquoise handles. And there was Aziz bringing his splendid slippers.

Rhamon looked down at his own beautiful ones and remembered the words Aziz had spoken, "Not even a king shall have a better pair."

At this moment the police boat nosed in toward the steps. Rhamon saw the chance he had been waiting for and reached for something hidden under the seat. He had no fine present to give; only a wreath of little yellow flowers he had made that morning.

As the Rajah stepped ashore Rhamon tossed the garland at his feet. The great man smiled a greeting to all his people. Then, seeing the wreath, he turned toward Rhamon and looking straight into his brown eyes, smiled again. Rhamon saw the great jewel sparkling on his turban and the strings of precious stones across his coat.

Then the Rajah walked slowly up the steps into the Palace followed by his officers. Gradually all the little boats turned and went on up the river. Rhamon sighed. The great day was over. But it had been one he would never forget. His dream had come true. The Rajah had smiled to him!

Chapter X

WONDERFUL NEWS

Several days later Rhamon was seated on the deck of the *Monarch* whittling out a top from a piece of hard root. Beside him sat the American Sahib, from whom he had borrowed the knife he was using. It was a beautiful knife—shiny and sharp—and the chips flew fast.

"Tell me more of the big cities, please, Sahib," said Rhamon.

The Sahib smiled and told him again of the

fine houses, the wide streets and the big steam trains that tore across the country and came puffing into the city stations.

Rhamon had heard many tales of the big cities on the other side of the mountains, but he had never seen them. The crumbling old city of Srinagar was the only one he knew. He had never been out of his valley that lay far up in the heart of the great mountains. In the winter the narrow mountain roads were often closed with snow. Then even the mail trucks could not come over them and the people in the high valley were shut off from news of the world below.

Rhamon's heart ached with the longing to be a man. He wanted to go down the mountains, to see the great cities and the steam trains.

So busy was Rhamon with his top and the stories which filled his ears, he did not notice that the sun was slowly sinking. As the fiery ball slipped behind the mountains it touched the plumy clouds with gold, and streaked the soft blue sky with rosy banners.

He bade the Sahib good-by and returning the knife, jumped into the *shikara* which lay alongside. This was the time of day Rhamon liked best. As he paddled the short distance to his own little houseboat, he watched the reflections in the river. One sun up in the sky, and one down there in the water!

Subro was resting on the tiny deck, smoking his hubble-bubble pipe. From the window drifted the spicy smell of curry. On the river bank close by, Rhamon's mother was pounding the rice. Thud—thud—thud! came the heavy sound of the pole as she let it fall. Rhamon could hear, the jingle-jingle of her many silver bracelets.

"Come here, Rhamon," said Subro, as the *shikara* drew alongside. "I have been waiting to speak with you."

Rhamon looked up quickly into his father's face. Was he to be scolded for staying away so long? But no, the brown eyes were smiling and kind. Rhamon tied the *shikara* and climbed up onto the deck.

"My son," began Subro, "you have long wanted to go down the mountains to the big city. And now I am going to send you. My brother lives in Lahore and owns a shop there. He has asked me to send him an old perfume jar. I have at last found the kind he wishes. You were with me when I bought it from Subhanna. Now you shall take it to your uncle. You are old enough to be trusted as a man."

Rhamon's heart thumped with joy and he felt that already he must have grown many inches—a man indeed!

"But that is not all," continued Subro, looking very tenderly at the happy face of his son. "On the day of the procession the good Rajah saw you and noticed your misfortune. And now he wishes to send you to the big city of Lahore. He believes the great doctor there will be able to make your foot right again, so that you can run like other boys."

"The Rajah!" exclaimed Rhamon breathlessly. He did not even hear what his father had

Subro was smoking his hubble-bubble pipe

told him about his foot. The Rajah, interested in him! But why?

Rhamon did not know of all that had happened since that wonderful day on the river. But the Chief of Police had told Subro many things. The Rajah had been pleased by the simple gift of the little boy. He had remembered the shining eyes and the bright smile. But he had also remembered Rhamon's crippled foot.

He had asked the Chief of Police the name of the boy who had been with him in the boat that day. And the Chief had told him how Rhamon had helped him catch the thieves.

All this Rhamon had not heard, and he stood there listening with open mouth and wondering happy eyes. "All because of my poor wreath," he thought.

"So now at last you are going to the big city, Rhamon," said his father. "The American Sahib and Mem Sahib leave in three days and you shall go with them. My brother will see that you return safely."

Chapter XI

A MOUNTAIN STORM

The day Rhamon started on his great adventure, the sky was dark and the rain was falling, falling. There was sunshine in his heart though, for was he not going to see the big city of his dreams? He hopped out of his father's *shikara* on the muddy river bank and waved good-by. By the time he reached the big automobile that was to take him down the mountains, his clothes were wet, and big clumps of red clay stuck to his sandals. But when he was settled in the front seat next to the friendly Indian driver, Rhamon was quite happy and he hugged the precious perfume jar tight in his arms. The Sahib and Mem Sahib climbed into the back and they were off.

This was Rhamon's first ride in a car, and he was so excited he could hardly sit still. Mile after mile they drove, along a wide road between two rows of tall green poplar trees. In the fields on each side peasants were working in the rice fields.

An hour passed and still it rained. They were climbing now and the mountain roads grew narrower and more winding. Rhamon looked at the great cliffs that stretched up and up on one side. Then he looked down on the other side at the Jhelum River that rushed along its noisy way, far, far below them.

It grew darker and darker. Lightning ripped the sky apart in blinding zigzag flashes. The pouring rain hammered against the car. Great claps of thunder shook the air and echoed

Lightning ripped the sky apart

through the valleys. The wind whistled and shrieked. Rhamon saw huge trees crash and tumble down the mountainsides.

Sometimes the car rushed dizzily around a narrow curve and up to the edge of nothing. Then Rhamon caught his breath and his heart stood still as he gazed through space. But before he knew it they were past the curve and safely on their way again.

At last the storm died away. The black clouds lifted, and the mountains, fresh washed, sparkled in the sunshine. Rhamon could see the flocks of long-haired goats scrambling up and up. High in the blue sky was a soaring eagle, on its way perhaps to some lonely mountain nest. Through the green valley down below ran the chattering river, foaming over the rocks. On the hillsides rested the pink and white clouds of blossoming fruit trees.

The car was climbing now, up and up into the mountains. The air grew colder and Rhamon snuggled down under a warm woolen blanket. Soon they reached the high Pir Panjal Pass between the mountains. Great peaks rose in silence above them. Patches of snow lay in the shadows.

Then they started down on the other side. As they went lower the air grew warmer, and Rhamon came out from under his blanket. The roads here were dusty, for it had not rained on this side of the pass. Rhamon grew thirsty. How he longed for a drink of the water that tumbled down in shining waterfalls!

Just then they whirled around a bend in the road. In front of them he saw a fairy spot where clear spring water fell like a sheet of sparkling rain. It dripped through a mass of green vines and hanging ferns. The car stopped and Rhamon sprang out. In a moment he was splashing the cool water on his face and drinking it from the cup of his hands.

While they rested there an old man wandered up to the car. His clothes were ragged and his white turban was covered with dust. In his hands he carried a queer little three-stringed instrument. Standing by the edge of the cliff he began to play.

As he drew his bow across the strings a sweet strange music filled the air. It told of fairies dancing in the moonlight, of running water, of springtime flowers and sunshine. Rhamon stood beside him and listened. Now the music sang of the loneliness of the mountains, of the coldness of their icy peaks, of cruel storms and of people lost.

Rhamon would have liked to stay longer, but he heard the Sahib calling his name, so he ran to the car and climbed into his seat. Soon they were driving down the narrow mountain road once more. The music of the strolling player was lost in the distance.

Chapter XII

THE FIRE-BREATHING MONSTER

As the car came lower and Rhamon breathed the hot dusty air of the plains he began to wish he were back in his lovely high valley where the air was cool and sweet. Now they began to pass oxcarts on the road. Small houses made of dried mud bricks were scattered here and there. People went riding by in jouncing little horse carts. Soldiers were to be seen lolling about everywhere. The long trip down the mountain was ended. They had reached the city.

It was sunset time when the car pulled up near the station in Rawal Pindi. The Sahib and Mem Sahib climbed out, stretched their legs and brushed off the thick white dust. Rhamon hopped out too, and looked at the sinking sun. He must hurry and say his prayers.

Placing the perfume jar in the Sahib's arms he ran to a street pump, splashed the water on his face and arms and washed off his feet. Then he saw, standing under a tree, another worshipper in the midst of his prayers. Rhamon knelt on the ground near him. Facing the Holy City he bowed his head to the ground many times and gave praise to Allah. And there was great thankfulness in his heart that he had come safely down the mountain.

"We will spend the night here in Rawal Pindi," said the Sahib, when they had finished their dinner. The next day when they went to take the train to Lahore, the station was crowded with people rushing this way and that, and carrying huge bundles. "Those bundles are their bedding rolls," the Sahib told Rhamon. "At night they are spread out on the seats, and in the daytime they are put back in those big bags."

Suddenly there was a shrill whistle, and down the track Rhamon saw a great light coming closer and closer. Surely it was the eye of some giant beast that was roaring and thundering toward him. The creature let out another sharp scream. It was almost on top of him, this huge black fire-breathing monster, with a tail that stretched far along the track. Then with a horrible noise it slowly stopped and stood there puffing and hissing and blowing great clouds of steam into the air. It had fire in its insides too, for Rhamon could feel the heat and see the blaze. This was Rhamon's first view of a railroad train.

"Come, Rhamon," said the Sahib, and gave Rhamon a boost up the steep steps into one of the coaches. People were leaning out of the windows, buying things to eat, or talking to friends. Passengers were crowding on with bags, bundles and bedding rolls.

For a minute Rhamon lost sight of the Sahib and Mem Sahib. Then he saw them again on ahead. Holding his perfume jar, he pushed his way down the aisle. Suddenly the train started. There was a terrific jerk and Rhamon found himself in a heap on the floor. When he had straightened his turban and looked around, the train was rumbling on its way. He was glad when the Sahib took his hand and led him to a seat.

The hot air was soon filled with smoke and cinders. The steady clackety-clack, clackety-clack, clackety-clack of the rolling wheels made Rhamon drowsy, and soon he was sound asleep, with his head resting against the Sahib's shoulder.

He knew nothing more till someone gently shook him. "This is Lahore. We get off here," said the Sahib.

Chapter XIII

RHAMON DELIVERS THE PERFUME JAR

Half-awake, Rhamon stumbled down the aisle. And then he remembered—he would see his uncle here. On the platform Rhamon was joggled and shoved about, and once his lovely turban was knocked down over his nose. He held tight to the Sahib's hand for fear he would lose him in the crowd.

Men were running along beside the train with trays of things to sell, balanced on their heads. Some were filled with fruits, others with pots of tea. Some were piled with long-handled fans of braided reeds or round ones made of bright peacock feathers. The Sahib stopped one of the men and bought Rhamon a little bag of candied pumpkin and a small red clay pot filled with sweet sticky cakes trimmed with tiny bits of beaten silver.

Suddenly Rhamon saw a tall man who looked like his father. He was glancing all about him as he came through the crowd. Then he saw Rhamon with the American Sahib and flashed them a smile. It was Rhamon's uncle who owned the shop in Lahore.

Now the American Sahib and the Mem Sahib were leaving, on another train. Already the porters were throwing their bags and bundles through the windows of one of the cars. Rhamon had just time to say good-by before the Sahib jumped on the moving train. Slowly it pulled out of the station snorting and blowing.

Rhamon watched, and waved to the Sahib, who was leaning out of the window. Then he turned and looked up into his uncle's smiling face. Hand in hand they walked out of the station. On the street his uncle hailed a *tonga* and they climbed into a small two-seated cart, pulled by a small and scraggy horse.

For some time they jogged along through the big old city, a part of the busy, bustling traffic. Rhamon looked about him on all sides. He had never seen such wide streets, such fine buildings, such well-dressed people, so many cars.

Then they passed through the great archway of one of the thirteen old city gates, and entered the native quarter. Here everything was different. Narrow dark little streets twisted this way and that. On each side as far as Rhamon could see there were high brick houses without windows, and endless rows of tiny shops.

Cows and bullocks wandered up and down the smelly crowded lanes, stopping to snatch a wisp of hay or nibble a vegetable at one of the market stalls. Loaded donkeys trotted past, squeaking oxcarts rumbled through the crowd, teams of water buffalo and flocks of sheep and goats took up the street. It was exciting and noisy and Rhamon loved it.

In front of the small shops sat the merchants. Here a potter was making his red clay jars, spinning the big wheel with a bare brown foot. Just beyond were men dyeing cloth in great kettles, and their arms were colored to the elbows. Across the way, standing side by side, were meat markets, gold- and silversmiths, fish stalls, basket shops, spice sellers and makers of sweetmeats. Some were bending over small charcoal fires. High up on a bluff he could see a great old fort—hundreds of years old, his uncle said. Rhamon could hardly wait to get out by himself. It would take him days, he thought, to explore all the wonderful sights.

In one of these crooked little lanes Rhamon's uncle had his shop. Here the *tonga* came to a halt and they both got out. The tiny window of the shop was filled with shining brass bowls and pots, trays and candlesticks. Inside were many shelves of beautiful things made of silver, copper and brass. Until this moment Rhamon had held on to the perfume jar, but now he handed it thankfully to his uncle who smiled and took off its many wrappings.

Truly it was a king among jars, tall and graceful and rich in color. Rhamon thought his uncle would never stop looking at it, tilting his head on one side and then on the other. At last he said, "Yes, the jar has great beauty. When you return, say to your father that he chose well. I have never seen one more perfect. It will please the prince for whom it was ordered." And he set it up in the window of his shop.

Chapter XIV

AN EXCITING DAY IN THE BAZAAR

The next morning Rhamon went with his uncle to see the city and buy some spices in the Bazaar. Rhamon had never seen such a big Bazaar. So, while his uncle was busy tasting and buying little bags of the strong, good-smelling spices, Rhamon slipped away.

He wandered up and down and looked into all the little shops and open stalls that lined the packed and winding streets. Here and there he stopped to watch a man sitting cross-legged on the ground, sewing or weaving, or hammering on a piece of metal. He listened to the bright-colored parrots that hung in cages by the doorways and called to the tame monkeys that swung along the railings or dropped down from roof tops. He poked the lazy dogs that slept in the hot dust or snapped at the buzzing flies.

Crowds of people passed him, coming and going in a steady stream. Some were dressed in bright silk, some were dressed in rags, but few of them wore clothes like the garments he knew at home in the Valley. No one noticed Rhamon and he ran about gayly, dodging the noisy little horse carts that rattled their way through the narrow busy streets.

Rhamon had some *annas* that jingled in his pockets, so he looked at the colored candies in this little shop, the sticky cakes in the next one, and the gay array of penknives in another. "I really need a penknife," he thought, "one with a sharp blade that will cut the hardest root.

Then I can whittle myself a top that *no one* can crack. I would like to have a knife like the American Sahib's." He remembered how he had once seen the Sahib cut a stick clear through with one slash of his beautiful knife. Ah, that was a knife worth having!

And so he stayed for a long time at this stall, looking first at one knife and then at another. But he could not find one like the Sahib's beautiful shiny knife that had come all the way from America.

As he went on through the Bazaar he saw a window full of wonderful tops. A splendid red and green one caught his eye, but he was sure it cost more than the four *annas* he had in his pocket. "I must bargain with this shopkeeper as the men do." So he went inside, looked at several tops and asked their price. Then he picked up the lovely red and green one and asked how much it was. "What! Seven *annas*? That is too much." So he put the top down and walked out of the store.

Crowds of people passed him coming and going

"Six *annas* for you, boy," the shopkeeper called after him.

Rhamon laughed to himself and thought, "I'm pretty good." He came back and looked at the top. "I will give you three *annas* for this top," he said, winding it up for a spin.

The shopkeeper threw up his hands in horror. "Three *annas*! And how shall a poor man live when he must sell his goods for so little? Oh woe, oh woe! I have no luck today." Then as Rhamon started for the door again, he called, "Five *annas* and the top is yours."

"I shall look at tops farther down the street," Rhamon answered, jingling the coins in his pocket. Now Rhamon wanted the top, so just as he reached the door he pulled out his money and said, "I will give you four *annas* for that top."

"Allah have mercy!" the old man muttered as he put the shiny top into Rhamon's hand and gathered up the four *annas* with his bony fingers.

But it would be hard to say who was the happier about the good bargain he had made, Rhamon or the shopkeeper.

At last Rhamon turned to go back to the stall where he had left his uncle buying spices. On the way he heard the sound of light fingers tapping on a drum, "Tum ta-ta tee tum; tum ta-ta tee tum." Quickly he wriggled his way through the small crowd of people that was gathered around the music. He ducked between the widespread legs of a brass peddler, nearly upsetting his tray of goods.

"You young rascal!" the old man screamed as he made a grab to catch Rhamon. But Rhamon was too quick for him and had safely hidden himself in front of a fat woman with a baby in her arms. Then he saw why the crowd was there.

A man was squatting on the sidewalk playing on a small drum. In front of him a young girl danced to his music and to the clink of the silver bells on her anklets. Her slender body swayed from side to side and her bare feet padded on the ground. Rhamon loved the music of her dancing feet. When she whirled, her skirts made a cloud of red and gold about her. A floating veil covered her face, so Rhamon could see only the flash of her great black eyes. Too soon the dance was ended and people tossed coins at her feet.

Rhamon wished he had not spent his last *anna* for that top. He would have liked to reach into his pocket and toss a coin to the pretty dancer just like the other men. However, he moved away to meet his uncle.

On the way home from the Bazaar Rhamon saw a man sitting on the ground, blowing fire out of his mouth. People were standing nearby watching him. Rhamon pulled his uncle's sleeve, "Look, the man is on fire!"

"O-ho," said his uncle, "we must stop here and watch him. He is Mohammed Bukhs, and he can do tricks that will make you think he must be made of magic."

All this time the trickster was puffing his

The trickster was making the flames shoot out from his lips

cheeks in and out, and in and out, like a pair of bellows, making the flames shoot out from his lips. Then he took the red coals out of his mouth and turned to his wife who was standing near him with a big basket.

Now for another trick. Rhamon watched him tie her hands together and fasten her inside of a strong rope net. Then he picked her up and stuck her feet first through a small hole in the top of the basket. She wriggled and squirmed her way down inside. Mohammed, the trickster, put a cloth over the hole. The basket began to wobble, then—out popped the net.

"Now how did she get out of that?" thought Rhamon.

At this moment Mohammed jumped into the basket with both feet and stamped about to show there couldn't be anybody inside. Where was his wife? Just to be sure she wasn't there he got out, and taking up a long sharp sword, plunged it into the basket, this way and that, in and out, again and again.

"What is happening to the poor lady inside?" asked Rhamon.

"Wait a moment and you will find out," said his uncle, who had seen the trick before.

Sure enough, the basket began to wriggle and roll from side to side. Then Mohammed's wife squeezed herself out through the top and stood there looking very hot but not the least bit hurt.

All the way home Rhamon thought about that trick, but he couldn't figure it out. With his own eyes he had seen the swords go through the basket, yet the man's wife was inside!

It had been a long and busy day for Rhamon and he was tired when he crawled into his little bed that night. His foot ached, and he thought how glad he would be if the good doctor was able to make it right, so he could walk and run without getting tired.

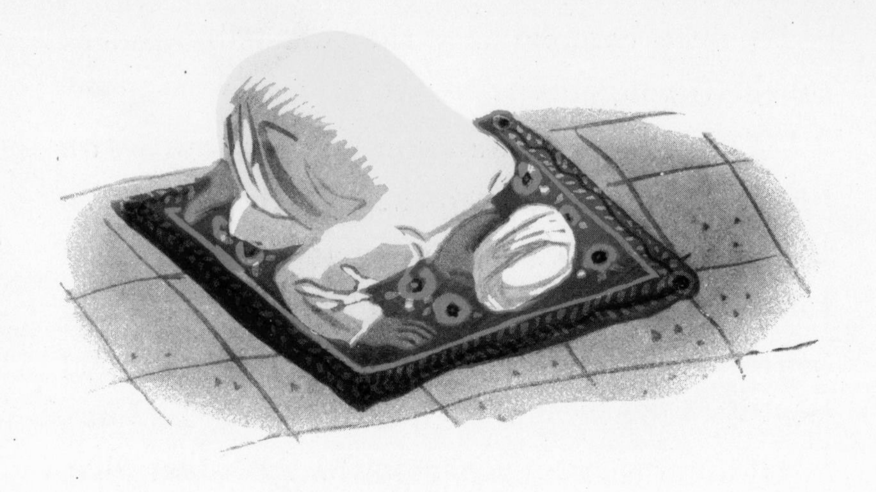

Chapter XV

SNAKE CHARMERS

Rhamon had learned to say his prayers at home with his father. Five times each day they said them, for they were good Mohammedans. Every morning at the break of day, every evening when the sun set, and three times in between, he faced the holy city of Mecca. Then kneeling down, he touched his forehead to the ground again and again, and gave praise to Allah.

But Rhamon had never been inside one of the big Mosques where Mohammedans go to pray. So when Friday came his uncle took him with him. All about the Mosque were beggars and cripples and blind people, and many with things to sell. Holding his uncle's hand, Rhamon passed through the splendid entrance, all covered with tiny blue, green, and orange stones.

In the courtyard were many people, some saying their prayers, others washing themselves. Rhamon and his uncle left their slippers beside a pool and like all the others bathed their faces and arms, then chests and feet. They must be clean before they prayed. Rhamon gazed up at the great dome sparkling in the sunlight and the high slender towers capped in gleaming gold.

"Soon," his uncle told him, "the Muezzin will come out on the top of one of those towers and you will hear him calling the faithful to their prayers."

It was as his uncle had said. While they stood there a tiny figure appeared high up on the tower. Then Rhamon heard a beautiful voice sing, *"Allah U Akbar! La-ee-la-ha Ill Allah!* There is but one God and Mohammed is his prophet." From every side people were coming to the Mosque in answer to his call.

Rhamon looked up and all he could see was the face and black beard of the Muezzin. "Ah, it must be fine," he thought, "to stand so far up there and sing like that! Some day I shall be a Muezzin and stand on a high tower to call the faithful to their prayers."

Then with all the other worshippers he entered the great Mosque. Each man went to his own special place to pray. Many had small rugs on which they kneeled. And all were facing in the same direction, toward the holy city of Mecca.

Soon the priest came, and standing in the small high pulpit led the prayers. Rhamon, kneeling on the prayer rug beside his uncle, prayed too, touching his head to the ground again and again. He listened to the great sound made by all the other praying voices, and his heart nearly burst.

Leaving the Mosque, Rhamon and his uncle made their way through the finest streets of the city to a great house with lovely gardens around it. "A rich prince lives here," said Rhamon's uncle. "He ordered the perfume jar you brought and now I am taking it to him."

As they came into the garden a sweet wailing music reached their ears. Rhamon stopped to listen. He had never heard anything like it before. Then he saw two men squatting on the grass not far off. They were wild-looking men with bold dark faces, and big black beards. Deep red turbans were twisted around their heads and yellow robes draped their brown bodies. They were playing on queer little flutes, while in front of them on the ground were two round baskets. As Rhamon came closer he noticed the big brass rings that swung from the men's ears and the many strings of beads around their necks.

"Those men are snake charmers," said his uncle. "Their fathers and grandfathers before them were snake charmers. They have a strange power over snakes. Even the most deadly one will not hurt them. And when they play their flutes the snakes must dance."

Rhamon listened and waited to see what would happen. Guests of the prince who had been walking in the garden now came over and gathered round the snake charmers to watch what they were doing.

The strange music of the flutes went on and on. Rhamon's eyes were fastened on the baskets. The music swelled and he saw the tops of the baskets slowly rise and fall to one side. A queer feeling arose in his stomach and he held tight to his uncle's hand. Then suddenly two snakes thrust their great heads out of the baskets. Slowly they uncoiled and waved back and forth. Rhamon could see their beady little eyes fixed on their masters.

As the music grew louder, one of the snakes

slid out of his basket and coiled up on the grass. He was many feet long. The snakes seemed to be under a magic spell and swayed in time with the music. Rhamon too was lost in the spell of the snake charmers.

Suddenly the music stopped and the snakes, free from its magic, started to glide away over the ground. With little cries the people scattered. But the two men were not afraid. They laughed, picked up the snakes and tucked them back into their baskets. Then they collected their money from the people who had gathered to watch them, salaamed, and in another moment were lost in the crowds of the streets.

Chapter XVI

ALL IS WELL FOR RHAMON

Rhamon was having such a good time visiting his uncle that he almost forgot the real reason he had come to Lahore. But one morning the great doctor arrived in the little brass shop.

"I have heard from the Rajah," he told Rhamon's uncle. "And now I have come to take this young man to the hospital."

A chill raced down Rhamon's spine. The hospital! But when he looked up and saw the kindly eyes smiling at him, he was no longer afraid. He put his hand into the big doctor's, and felt quite willing to go with him anywhere, even to the hospital.

"You are in good hands, Rhamon," said his uncle. "You have nothing to fear." Then he gave Rhamon a small flat box. "It is a present from the American Sahib. He told me to give it to you the day that you went to the hospital."

Rhamon tore open the box and there lay the thing he had most wished for — the beautiful American penknife! "This will be my good-luck," he thought, and with a sigh of happiness, put it into his pocket.

Everything about the hospital was strange to Rhamon, the clean strong smell of the place, the nurses, the doctors, and the high bed with the white sheets, on which he slept. But his bright smile won him many friends and soon he felt quite happy.

The next day, the doctor said he must operate on Rhamon's foot. The nurses wheeled him into the special room where the big doctor stood ready, all dressed in white.

But Rhamon was not afraid. "See, I have my good-luck with me," he said, smiling and opening his hand to show the doctor his American penknife.

"Yes, you are right," said the doctor, smiling too. "Your good-luck will be with you." The nurse put a mask over his face and told him to breathe deep. A queer smell filled his nostrils. After that, Rhamon did not know anything more till he found himself back in bed with his foot wrapped up in yards and yards of bandages.

For many days he stayed in the hospital, but when he finally left with his uncle, he walked out on two good solid feet, as good and strong as any boy's in India!

"I think my penknife did bring me good luck," said Rhamon reaching into his pocket to make sure it was still there.

"Yes, perhaps it did," said his uncle, "but you must not forget to give thanks to Allah, for the kindness of the Rajah and the skill of the great doctor."

Rhamon nodded his head and walked on, glad to be out again in the fresh air and sunshine.

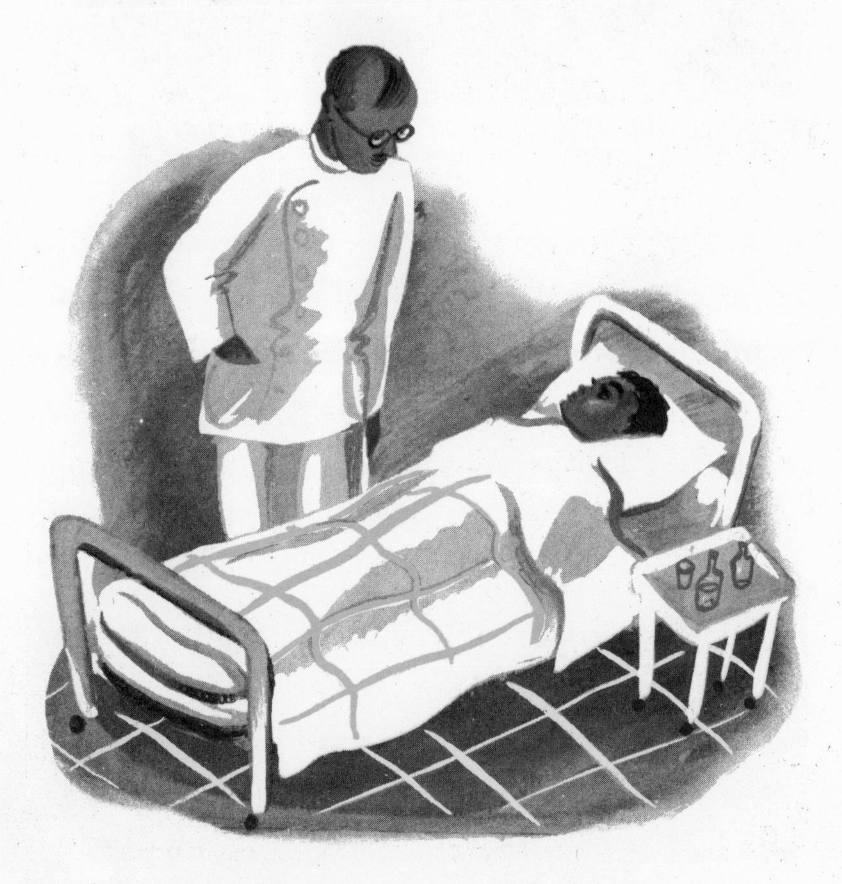

Chapter XVII

GOING HOME WITH THE ROAD GANG

All too soon the day arrived for Rhamon to start home again. He went back to Rawal Pindi with his uncle, and there he was put in the care of a gang of workmen who were being sent up into the mountains to repair the roads. In one place a bridge had been washed away by the heavy rains. In another, mud and rocks had fallen down onto the roads from the high cliffs overhead. There were nearly a hundred men in the gang and they traveled in heavy covered carts pulled by sleepy-looking oxen. The lumbering animals traveled slowly and rested often, for the roads were steep.

At night the oxen were unhitched and lay down beside the carts. Then Rhamon liked to help the men take the sweet-smelling hay from the lower parts of the wagons and feed the animals. After they were fed, fires were built all along the road and the men cooked their evening meal.

Rhamon ate with them and listened to their talk. When his eyes grew heavy he crept under his covers in the top part of one of the wagons. Then he drifted off to sleep hearing the friendly crackle of the fires, the low voices of the men and the soft breathing of the oxen.

After seven days of travel like this the workmen reached the spot where the bridge was broken. Here the big mail-truck had been stopped on its way down. And here Rhamon said good-by to the workmen who had become his friends. They had brought the mail up this far with them, and Rhamon was to go on the rest of the way with the mail truck which would turn back now to Srinagar.

When he finally reached Srinagar and jumped down from the mail truck he saw the tall, white-robed figure of his father, waiting to meet him. Subro picked Rhamon up off his feet and gave him a great hug, then set him down again, saying over and over again, "Allah be praised! Allah be praised!"

Just as they stepped into Subro's *shikara* to paddle home, the Chief of Police rushed up, the end of his great turban flying in the breeze. He slapped Rhamon on the back, then rubbed his big nose and twirled his black moustache. "Now you will surely be a Chief of Police!" he shouted, "and not a thief shall escape you!"

Then as the boat pulled away Rhamon heard him begin to laugh—that hearty laugh which he was sure always started away down in the the tips of his uncle's red leather slippers.

Subro picked Rhamon up in his arms

When Rhamon climbed out on the deck of his own houseboat his mother put her arm around him. For a long time she didn't say anything. Wasn't she glad to see him? Under her long black lashes he couldn't tell whether she was laughing or crying. But that night when she cooked supper and he sat on the little rug in the corner listening to her singing, he thought she sounded happier than ever before.

After they had all eaten their evening meal Rhamon told Subro and his mother of the many wonderful sights he had seen in the big city: the snorting steam train, the great Mosque where he had said his prayers, the busy Bazaar with its hundreds of shops, the strange men who charmed the poison snakes, and his trip up the mountains with the gang of workmen.

Before he went to sleep he tucked his beautiful American penknife under his pillow. After all it was good to be home again on his houseboat — to see the stars from his window and the lights of the little Temple on the hill.

As the days passed, Rhamon grew and learned to do all the things that the men could do. He helped his father with the houseboats. He learned to work in the market gardens, to gather driftwood in the river, to swim, to fish, and to hunt.

Some day Rhamon will be a man. Then he will have a long black beard. He will wear rustling white garments and smoke a big water pipe. Perhaps he will be the Rajah's head boatman, perhaps he will be a Chief of Police. And perhaps he will own fine houseboats on the river like his father.

KASHMIRI WORDS

Srinagar	S(u)r-in-ag′-ar
Rhamon	Rhä-mōn
Subro	Soo′-bro
chupatti	chu-pät-tĭ
shikara	shĭ-kä′-rȧ
tonga	tŏng-gȧ

Pronunciation

ä as in far
ȧ as in Vera
oo as in moon
ĭ as in tin
u as in pull
o as in cot